41

KING ROLLO'S LETTER

AND OTHER STORIES

D1581238

ALSO AVAILABLE IN RED FOX BY DAVID McKEE

KING ROLLO'S LETTER

AND OTHER STORIES

KING ROLLO AND THE LETTER
KING ROLLO AND THE BUSH
KING ROLLO AND THE PRESENT
KING ROLLO AND THE TENT

RED FOX

A Red Fox Book

Published by Random House Children's Books
20 Vauxhall Bridge Road, London SW1V 2SA
A division of The Random House Group Ltd
London Melbourne Sydney Auckland
Johannesburg and agencies throughout the world

1 3 5 7 9 10 8 6 4 2

First published by Andersen Press 1984
Beaver edition 1986
Red Fox edition 2000

Printed in Hong Kong

The RANDOM HOUSE Group Limited Reg. No. 954009
www.randomhouse.co.uk

ISBN 0 09 947610 X

KING ROLLO
and the letter

King Rollo looked out of his window and watched as the postman went past.

"Huh!" he said. "The postman never brings me any letters."

"You never write any letters," said the magician. "You can't expect to get letters if you don't send any."

"I'll write a letter today," said King Rollo and he ran off to get writing things.

Then he settled down and began to write a letter.

"Come and play in the garden," said Queen Gwen. "It's a lovely day."

"I have to finish this letter first," said King Rollo, frowning. "I can't think what to say."

"Say that you are going to play with me," said Queen Gwen.

King Rollo thought and then wrote some more.

Then he went to the magician. "What can I write in my letter?" he asked.

"Write that I am inventing a new spell," said the magician.

King Rollo was interested. "What does it do?" he asked.

"It makes people vanish when they bother me," said the magician.

King Rollo left. "It works," chuckled the magician.

"What can I put in my letter?" King Rollo asked Cook.

"You can say that you're going to have jelly for tea," said Cook. "Oh good," said King Rollo.

"And a bath this evening," added Cook.
"Oh bad," said King Rollo.

When he could think of nothing else to
write about, King Rollo put the letter in
an envelope.

Queen Gwen went with King Rollo to
post the letter.

Afterwards they went back and played
ball in the garden.

The next day King Rollo looked out of the window. "Here comes the postman," he said.

"Be patient," said the magician. "You only wrote yesterday, you can't expect a letter yet."

"Oh yes I can," laughed King Rollo, as he ran to collect the letter.

"That letter that I wrote yesterday, I sent to myself."

KING ROLLO and the bush

"I think I'll buy a bush to plant in the garden," said King Rollo.

"Well, make sure you plant it properly," said the magician. "And don't get anything too big," said Cook.

When King Rollo came out of the shop he met Queen Gwen.

"I've just bought a bush for the garden," he said.

"It's not very big," said Queen Gwen. "It will soon grow," said King Rollo.

"I'll come and see how it looks later," said Queen Gwen.

The magician was in the garden when King Rollo returned.

"That's not very big," he said, looking at the plant. "It will soon grow," said King Rollo.

King Rollo started to dig a hole for the bush.

"I know I said not too big but that really is small," said Cook. "It will soon grow," said King Rollo.

King Rollo looked at the little bush and thought.

Cook was busy in the kitchen when King Rollo came in with a watering can.

"I just need some water for the bush," he explained.

"It needs more than water," said Cook. "Perhaps I'd better go and look at it."

When King Rollo took the water into the garden, the magician, Cook and Queen Gwen were all standing together.

Where the little bush had been there was now a big bush.

"I can't believe my eyes," said Cook.

"He did say it would grow," said Queen Gwen.

"He must have been using my book of magic spells," said the magician, "and that is very naughty."

"What do you mean?" said King Rollo.

"It's grown so quickly," said the magician.

"Well," smiled King Rollo. "You did all moan that it was too small."

"Anyway, I didn't use magic," he said. "I bought a bigger bush."

"The small one is over there, and it will soon grow."

KING
ROLLO
and the
present

"King Frank is ill," said Cook. "Why don't you take him a present to cheer him up?"

"That's a good idea," said King Rollo and he went to the shop.

In the shop King Rollo looked for something to amuse King Frank.

Finally he chose a cowboy on a horse that jumped up and down after it was wound up.

King Rollo took the present to show Cook.

"Very nice," said Cook. "Now put it away or you will break it."

"I'll just try it out," said King Rollo. He wound up the horse and put it on the table.

"Lovely," said Cook as the horse jumped about. "Now put it away."

"Just one more go," said King Rollo. Then before he could stop it the horse jumped off the table.

"Now look what you've done," said Cook, pointing at the broken horse.

"It wasn't made strongly enough," said King Rollo. "I'll get the magician to mend it."

"It needs a magic spell," said King Rollo. "It needs care and patience," said the magician.

After a while he said, "There, it's as good as new. Let's try it out."

He wound up the horse and let it jump about. "Perfect," said King Rollo. "I'll put it back in the box."

"We'll have one more go," said the magician. "It's rather fun." He wound the horse up again.

This time the horse jumped right off the edge of the bench.

"Now look what you've done! You've broken it again," said King Rollo.

"It wasn't made strongly enough," said the magician. "What it needs is a little magic." And he made a spell.

The horse looked like new. "Now it really is better than new," said the magician.

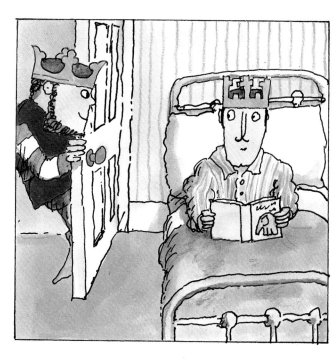

That afternoon King Rollo visited King Frank.

"I've brought you a present to make you feel better," said King Rollo.

"Thank you, that looks fun," said King Frank. "Let's try it."

"The magician has made it specially strong," said King Rollo. "Just in case …

… you have an accident."

KING ROLLO
and the
tent

King Rollo was in the garden when King Frank arrived. "I've brought my tent," he said.

They took the tent out of its bag and started to put it up. It wasn't easy.

"What are you doing?" asked Cook. "Putting up King Frank's tent," said King Rollo.

"Well, be careful," said Cook.

When the tent was ready they both went into it.

Then they came out again. "Are you going to sleep in it?" asked the magician.

"Pardon?" said King Frank. The magician laughed. "I asked if you are going to sleep in the tent."

"What a good idea," said King Rollo. "Let's tell Cook." And they ran indoors.

"King Frank is going to stay the night and we're going to sleep in the tent," said King Rollo.

"Oh dear, it's getting very windy," said Cook.

"You're right," said King Rollo. "We'll need to move the tent. Come on, King Frank."

"Sleep in the tent? Oh dear!" said Cook. "Don't worry, we'll keep an eye on them," said the magician.

King Rollo and King Frank rushed about with blankets and things. They could hardly wait for bedtime.

At last they took their bedtime drinks and said "Goodnight" to Cook and the magician.

"I hope you'll be warm enough," said Cook. "Of course we will, stop worrying," said King Rollo.

But Cook did worry. "I can't see anything in the dark," she said. "I hope they're all right."

"Of course they are," said the magician.
'But we'll look outside if you like."

They went outside. "I can't see the tent,"
said the magician. "It was here
somewhere."

"They said they were going to move it,"
said Cook as they kept looking.

When they still couldn't find it, they
called out, "King Rollo, where are you?"

Suddenly one of the palace windows opened. "What's all that shouting?" King Rollo called.

Cook and the magician stared in surprise. "We thought you were going to sleep in the tent," said Cook.

"We are, but not out there in the cold, silly," said King Rollo.

"We moved the tent to the playroom, and if you don't mind we are going back to bed. Goodnight."